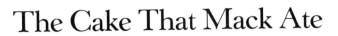

The Cake That Mack Ate

To Darrell
He takes the cake

Text Copyright © 1986 by Rose Robart
Illustrations Copyright © 1986 by Maryann
Kovalski

First American Edition

Library of Congress Catalog Card No. 86-47709

ISBN 0-316-74890-0

10 9 8 7 6 5 4

First published in Canada by Kids Can Press
Printed by Everbest Printing Co., Ltd., Hong Kong

The Cake That Mack Ate

WRITTEN BY **Rose Robart**

ILLUSTRATED BY **Maryann Kovalski**

Little, Brown and Company

Boston   Toronto   London

This is the cake
that Mack ate.

This is the egg
That went into the cake
that Mack ate.

This is the hen
That laid the egg,
That went into the cake
that Mack ate.

This is the corn
That fed the hen,
That laid the egg,
That went into the cake
that Mack ate.

This is the seed
That grew into corn,
That fed the hen,
That laid the egg,
That went into the cake
 that Mack ate.

This is the farmer
Who planted the seed,
That grew into corn,
That fed the hen,
That laid the egg,
That went into the cake
that Mack ate.

This is the woman
Who married the farmer,
Who planted the seed,
That grew into corn,
That fed the hen,
That laid the egg,
That went into the cake
  that Mack ate.

These are the candles
That lit up the cake,
That was made by the woman,
Who married the farmer,
Who planted the seed,
That grew into corn,
That fed the hen,
That laid the egg,
That went into the cake
    that Mack ate.

This is Mack . . .

He ate the cake.